NIKKI GRIMES
OH, BROTHER!
Illustrations by Mike Benny

Amistad

GREENWILLOW BOOKS
An Imprint of HarperCollinsPublishers

For Jarius and Jaraya—N.G.

For Mom and Dad—M.B.

Oh, Brother!
Poems copyright © 2008 by Nikki Grimes
Amistad is an imprint of HarperCollins Publishers, Inc.
Illustrations copyright © 2008 by Mike Benny
All rights reserved. Manufactured in China.
www.harpercollinschildrens.com

Gouache paints were used to prepare the full-color art.
The text type is Egyptian505.

Library of Congress Cataloging-in-Publication Data
Grimes, Nikki.
Oh, Brother! / by Nikki Grimes;
illustrations by Mike Benny.
  p. cm.
"Greenwillow Books."
Summary: Xavier is unhappy when his mother
remarries and he suddenly has a new stepbrother,
as well as a stepfather, in his home.
ISBN-13: 978-0-688-17294-7 (trade bdg.)
ISBN-10: 0-688-17294-6 (trade bdg.)
ISBN-13: 978-0-688-17295-4 (lib. bdg.)
ISBN-10: 0-688-17295-4 (lib. bdg.)
[1. Stepfamilies—Fiction. 2. Brothers—Fiction.
3. Remarriage—Fiction. 4. Hispanic Americans—Fiction.]
I. Benny, Mike, (date), ill. II. Title.
PZ7.G88429Om 2007 [E]—dc22 2005035645

First Edition 10 9 8 7 6 5 4 3 2 1

 Greenwillow Books

OH, BROTHER!

Mami remarried
and won me a brother.
"Don't need one," I said.
"But thanks, anyway."
Guess what? She ignored me!
Chris moved in today.

TROUBLE

"Three is company.
Four is a crowd."
Mami glared at me.
(I said that out loud?)

I had my reasons.
Things were just great
when Mami, me, and stepdad-to-be
would go on a date

for dinner, or movies.
Or, when we'd go alone,
cruising video arcades,
two men on our own.

Then, one night he brings
his son, Chris, along!
The earth lost its axis
and spun around wrong.

Chris grinned over pizza,
cut Mami a thick slice.
I groaned when she said,
"Now, wasn't that nice?"

Mami says he's lonely—
like I really care!
If he plans to steal her,
he'd better beware!

MOUSE

Two new bodies
carving up my space.
Four new feet
stomping round this place.
Two new voices
ringing through the house.
There won't be room
for me unless
I turn into a mouse!

STEPS

Everyone in this house
is a step, now.
Stepmom.
Stepdad.
Stepson.
Stepbrother.

In my mind,
I turn them into steps
I can climb.
And when I reach
the top,
I rule.

IMITATION
BROTHER

We walk to school
but not together.
Chris takes one street,
I take another.
No way will I ever
call him brother.
He doesn't even know
how to spell my name.

SMILE, CHRIS

Flash me that fake smile
the way you do whenever
your dad's in the room.

PLAY BALL

It's Saturday.
Chris is outside
burning up home plate,
skinning the brick wall
with his fastball.
Thwap!
He's mad at my stepdad,
who's busy pushing papers,
not on the pitcher's mound.

But wait!
What's that sound?
It's Mami,
spitting into her mitt.
"Come on. Let's do it, *hijo*,"
she says.
Chris ducks his head
to hide a smirk.
Uh-oh. He's in trouble now!

"What? You think I can't play?
Listen. I struck your dad out
three times in a row
at the company picnic.
That's how we met, *hijo*.
He had to know
who this girl was
showing him up.
So come on."

Chris tossed her a curve,
then *Wham!*
She zinged that ball
back so fast,
it knocked him on his—
Well, I watched
through the screen door,
smiling at Mami.
Proud.

PERFECT

I know he's up to something.
I've watched him ever since
he's started taking on my chores
like Mami's little prince.

Each night, he clears the table,
revved up like a machine,
then speed-scrubs every greasy dish
until it's squeaky clean.

He shows his dad his homework
without a smudge in sight.
Somehow he even calculates
those dumb math problems right.

If our bedtime is 8:15,
his eyes are closed by 8:00.
So when I crawl in bed on time,
it seems as if I'm late.

This kid is making me look bad.
He's perfect as a clock.
Dios! I wish he'd disappear.
Tick tock, tick tock, tick . . .

SHOWDOWN

One night, we're nose to nose.
Fists tight, I glare at Chris.
No dragon breathes as hot as me.
I've had enough of this!

"I'm sick of Mr. Perfect!
 Just be a normal kid!"
"I can't," Chris says, then rubs his eye.
 What's leaking from the lid?

"Oh, man. Don't do that, Chris.
 Look, all I'm saying is
 I'd sure like you a whole lot more
 if you weren't such a whiz."

"Unless I'm perfect," whispers Chris,
"my dad might go away.
 Normal wasn't good enough
 to make my mama stay."

The sprinkler system in his eyes
switches on full blast.
The fiery anger in my heart
sputters . . . out at last.

DREAM MOM

Chris says his mother is like a ghost. He only sees her in his dreams.

BEDTIME

Mami tucks us in
like always.
She kisses us good night,
switches off the light,
but not before Chris says,
"Good night, Mom."
He's ready to own her now.
Part of me thinks
that's okay.
Part of me wishes
he'd go away.

PHOTOGRAPH

Papi's smiling face—
the only part of him
I can trace.
73 cities away,
he calls sometimes.
I jerk the telephone cord
like rope.
Hold on, Papi.
I take a deep breath
and pull,
drawing him back to me

Sure, I can see
it's better now,
him gone,
and no more screaming
at Mami.
Pero, I miss Papi.
Does that sound dumb?
"Nah," says Chris.
"He's your dad.
You gotta miss him, some."

LIGHTS OUT

Sometimes
late at night,
hours after
the last lights wink out,
Chris and I
trade jokes
and line the walls
with laughter.

BASEBALL SURPRISE

I want to play like A-Rod.

I want to own home plate.

One thing has always

stopped me, though.

My batting doesn't rate.

That's about to change.

I'll see a ball, and *POW!*

I'll send it clear

round Saturn's rings.

My *brother*

taught me how.

THE NAME GAME

Chris and his notebook
deep in conversation.
Why the concentration?
"X-A-V-I-E-R," he spells.
I peek over his shoulder,
gasp at the number of *Xaviers*
staring from his page.
"What're you doing?"
"Practicing," Chris says.
"Until I get it right."
"Well, you got it wrong."
"What?"
I swipe his pen
and write H-E-R-M-A-N-O.
"Huh?" Chris can be slow.
"It means brother," I say.
"That's my name now,
one you already know how
to spell."

MAMI

Mami has a new happy
on her face.
When Chris and I
wrestle for fun,
she's the first one
grinning,
licking us
like scoops of ice cream
with her eyes.

NEWS

First, we huddled outside their door,

pondering what they'd called us for.

"We're moving to a larger place—"

"Where you and me will have more space!"

"As soon as we hear their big surprise—"

"Let's drop our jaws and widen our eyes!"

So we went in. I hid my smile.

My stepfather coughed. Mami giggled awhile.

They looked at each other, and then both spoke.

"We're having a baby." Is this some joke?

"In this house, *mijos*, we tell no lies.

Now close your mouths, or you'll catch flies!"

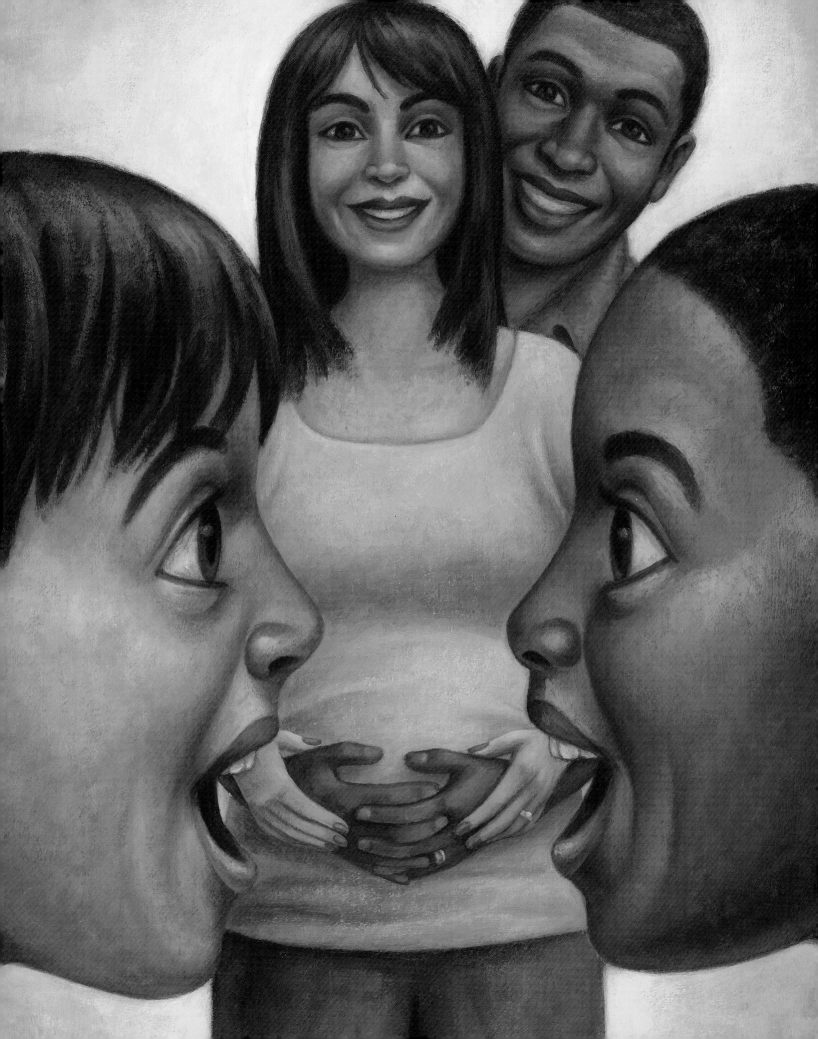

IT

Its eyes are oceans.
It smells like milk,
slides like an eel,
feels like silk.
It grabs Chris's finger,
before it turns to me.
Then Mami says, "*Hijos*,
meet your sister, Melodye."

A NEW SONG

After this year,
I've learned one thing:
Our family
is a song we sing,
and we can add new notes
anytime we like.

PACT

Chris and I decide:

No matter what, we're brothers.

And nobody leaves.